W9-DAJ-702

Big Problem

DISCARD

CARAMEL TREE

Chapter 1

A BIG Problem

Judy is at the hospital.
She waits to see the doctor.

"The doctor will see you now,"
says the nurse.

Judy sits on a bench.
"Hello, Judy," says the doctor.

"What is wrong?" asks the doctor.
"I have a BIG problem," says Judy.

Chapter 2 — I See!

"I see," says the doctor.
"What do you see?" asks Judy.

"Do you have a headache?" asks the doctor.
"No, I do not have a headache," says Judy.

"Do you have a cold?" asks the doctor.
"No, I do not have a cold," says Judy.

"Do you have a tummy problem?" asks the doctor.

"No, I do not have a tummy problem," says Judy.

"Do you have a runny nose?" asks the doctor.

"No, I do not have a runny nose," says Judy.

"Well," says the doctor.
Judy wants to cry. "What?" she asks.

The doctor looks at Judy's eyes.
"My eyes are okay," says Judy.

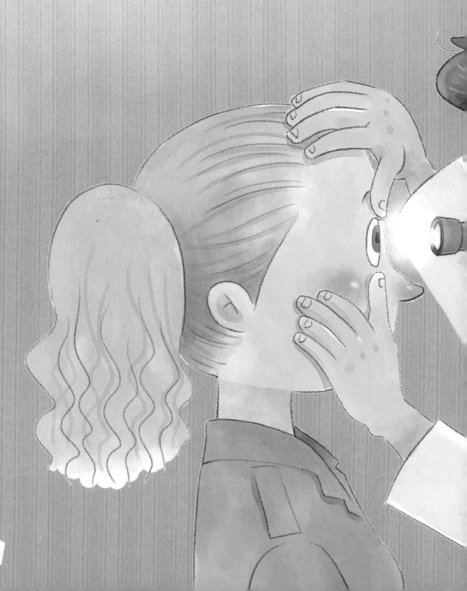

The doctor looks at Judy's ears.

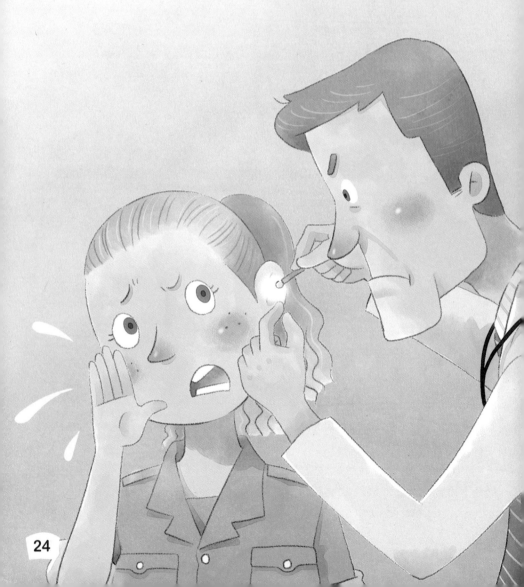

"My ears are okay," says Judy.

The doctor looks at Judy's nose.

"My nose is okay," says Judy.

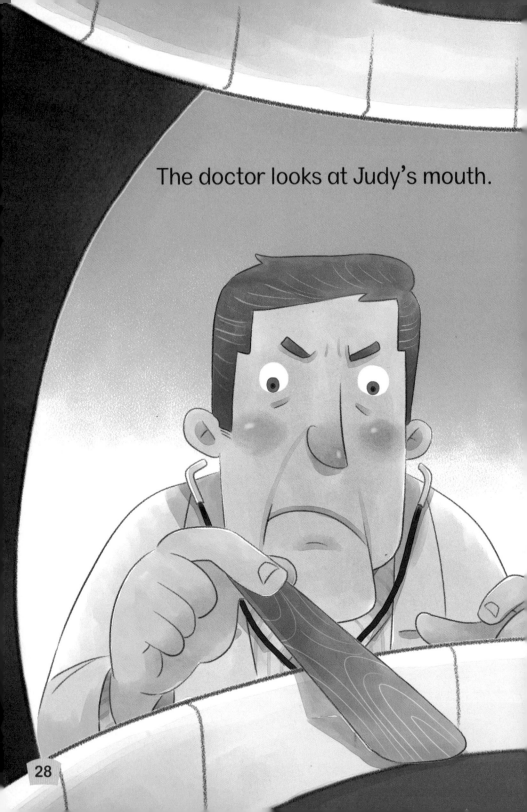

The doctor looks at Judy's mouth.

"My mouth is okay," says Judy.

The doctor holds Judy's neck.
"My neck is okay," says Judy.

The doctor holds Judy's arms.
"My arms are okay," says Judy.

"Aha!" says the doctor. "You have the flu!"

"I do not have the flu," says Judy.

"An elephant sat on my foot!" says Judy.